THE
RAINBOW GOBLINS

Ul de Rico
THE RAINBOW GOBLINS

WARNER BOOKS

A Warner Communications Company

Once there was a land that lived in fear of seven goblins. They were called the Rainbow Goblins and each had his own colour, which was also his name: Red, Orange, Yellow, Green, Blue, Indigo and Violet. Yellow, being the craftiest, was their chief. The goblins lived on colour—they prowled the valleys and climbed the highest mountains looking for rainbows, and when they found one, they caught it in their lassoes, sucked the colours out of it and filled their bellies with its bright liquid.

Only one place in the land had never known goblin-fear—the hidden valley called the Valley of the Rainbow, where the great arches of colour were born. There the animals still lived in paradise.

But the Rainbow Goblins had heard tales of this Valley, and their mouths watered whenever they thought of the feast that awaited them there; and so they gathered up their lassoes and their pails and set off.

With great effort, the goblins made their way over the jagged piles of rock that guarded the entrance. When the climbing became difficult, Yellow roared: "Don't lose heart comrades! Think of the delicious colours ahead!"

The sun had almost set by the time they reached their goal—the very meadow where the Rainbow sprang to life. Immediately beneath the meadow they found a cave. "We'll spend the night here," the Yellow Goblin commanded.

When the moon rose and saw them warming themselves around the fire they had lit, it shouted out in alarm: "The Rainbow Goblins are in the Valley!" The trees and the bushes took up the cry, and the flowers and the grasses and the animals and the waters passed it on, and by midnight the evil tidings had spread throughout the Valley.

The goblins could hardly contain their excitement. "Soon all the colours of the Rainbow will be ours," Yellow gloated. "We'll snatch it as it rises," said Green, "when the colours are still fresh and creamy." The Blue Goblin cackled, "Look at the roots dangling from the walls. They're straining to hear our plans. A lot of good it will do them, or their friend the Rainbow."

Finally, exhausted by their scheming, the goblins fell asleep. Outside, the moon shone on the mirror-like surface of the water, and its magical light was reflected into the cave.

Then all seven goblins had a wonderful dream—the same wonderful dream about the paradise of Rainbowland, where all you had to do was lie on your back and open your mouth, and the most succulent colours dripped down your throat.

The dream went on and on, the greedy goblins drank and drank, and at dawn, just as their bellies were about to burst, they were awakened by a distant clap of thunder.

The goblins sprang to their feet and rushed to the mouth of the cave. "A storm, a storm!" Red shouted. "Look how the wind is driving it toward us!" Orange cried.

And all the goblins danced and pranced about in glee, for they knew that after the wildest morning thunderstorm comes the most beautiful rainbow.

Yellow was so proud of his plan of attack that he went over it again, while each goblin tested his lasso. "Red, don't forget that you must seize the left flank." "And I move in on the right," the Violet Goblin burst out excitedly. Before the last roll of thunder had faded from the Valley the goblins took up their pails and lassoes and marched single file out of the cave.

The sight that greeted them when they reached the meadow took their breath away. The rising arch of the Rainbow, so rich with colour and promise, almost blinded them. Trembling with excitement, Yellow finally managed to give the signal to attack.

The goblins swung their lassoes around and around, and hurled them into the sky. But in that same instant the Rainbow vanished, as if it had been swallowed up by the earth. The goblins were dumbfounded. Nothing like this had ever happened to them before. They stared up at their empty outstretched lassoes...

...which a second later snapped back at them. Indigo wept, Blue cursed, Yellow stumbled, Orange cried out, "Treachery!" Violet tumbled to the grass, Red raged; but the more they thrashed about, the more tangled up they became in their own lassoes, until they had snarled themselves into a grunting, groaning mass of goblins on the ground.

As they lay there helplessly, a flood of colours poured forth from all the flowers of the meadow. "The flowers," screamed the Blue Goblin, "the flowers!" He had suddenly remembered the dangling roots he had made fun of in the cave. Through their roots the flowers had heard the goblins' plans, and they had devised a counter-plan to save the Rainbow. The moment the attack was launched, the flowers had drained the colours of the Rainbow into their petals, and as soon as the goblins became ensnared in their own lassoes, the petals had let loose the deluge.

So the goblins drowned in the colours they had come to steal, and no one in the Valley wept for them.

The Rainbow itself was reborn more magnificently than ever. Out of gratitude, it lifted up the flowers that had saved it and transformed them into glittering dragonflies and butterflies and splendidly plumed birds.

But since that time the Rainbow has become more cautious. Now when it arches across the sky it is careful not to touch the earth anywhere. No matter how you try to sneak up on it, you can never come to the place where it begins or ends.

Ul de Rico, otherwise Count Ulderico Gropplero di Troppenburg, was born in 1944 in Udine, Italy, and has lived for many years in Munich. He received his artistic education at the Munich Academy, where he first studied painting under Professor Franz Nagel and eventually took his graduate diploma in stage and costume design under the direction of Professor Rudolf Heinrich. For some years he has devoted himself almost exclusively to portrait painting.

This Warner Books Edition is published by arrangement
with Thames and Hudson Inc.

Warner Books, Inc., 666 Fifth Avenue, New York,
N.Y. 10103

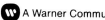 A Warner Communications Company

Printed in the United States of America

First Printing: October 1979
Reissued: November 1983

10 9 8 7 6 5 4 3

Library of Congress Cataloging in Publication Data

Da Rico, Ul, 1944–
  The rainbow goblins.

  Translation of Die Regenbogenkobolde.
  SUMMARY: After seven goblins try to steal it, the Rainbow
is careful never again to touch the earth.
  [1. Rainbow—Fiction.   2. Fairies—Fiction]
1. Title.
PZ7.D4425Rai 1979   [E]   79-13625
ISBN 0-446-37928-X (USA)
ISBN 0-446-37929-8 (Canada)